Tell Me Why

WHY?

We Have Earthquakes

Linda Crotta Brennan

Published in the United States of America by Cherry Lake Publishing
Ann Arbor, Michigan
www.cherrylakepublishing.com

Content Adviser: Jack Williams, science writer specializing in weather
Reading Adviser: Marla Conn, ReadAbility, Inc.

Photo Credits: © Pete Pahham/ Shutterstock Images, cover, 1, 5; © Dalton Dingelstad/ Shutterstock
Images, cover, 1, 15; © Digital Media Pro/ Shutterstock Images, cover, 1, 9; © fotostory/ Shutterstock
Images, cover, 1, 5; © Darren J. Bradley/ Shutterstock Images, cover, 1, 11; © Tom Wang/ Shutterstock
Images, cover, 1, 17; © michaeljung/ Shutterstock Images, back cover; © Lindwa/Shutterstock Images, 7;
© Vitoriano Junior/Shutterstock Images, 9; © mstay/iStock, 13; © jamesbenet/iStock, 15; © bluecrayola/
Shutterstock Images, 19; © daulon/Shutterstock Images, 21

Library of Congress Cataloging-in-Publication Data

Brennan, Linda Crotta, author.
  We have earthquakes / by Linda Crotta Brennan.
    pages cm. -- (Tell me why)
  Summary: "Offers answers to the most compelling questions about natural
disasters and the earth's crust. Age-appropriate explanations and appealing
photos. Additional text features and search tools, including a glossary and
an index, help students locate information and learn new words"-- Provided
by publisher.
  Audience: Grade K to 3.
  Includes bibliographical references and index.
  ISBN 978-1-63188-011-7 (hardcover) -- ISBN 978-1-63188-054-4 (pbk.) --
ISBN 978-1-63188-097-1 (pdf) -- ISBN 978-1-63188-140-4 (ebook) 1.
Earthquakes--Juvenile literature--Miscellanea. 2. Children's questions and
answers--Miscellanea. I. Title.

QE521.3.B74 2015
551.22--dc23

2014005710

Cherry Lake Publishing would like to acknowledge the work of The Partnership for 21st Century Skills.
Please visit *www.p21.org* for more information.

Printed in the United States of America
Corporate Graphics Inc.

Table of Contents

Rattling Snack

Keko sat down for her after-school snack. Suddenly, her plate started rattling. Her milk spilled. Duffy whined and scooted under the table.

Keko reached down and stroked her dog. He was shaking.

"That was strange," she said.

Her dad came in. "We just had an earthquake!" he said.

"What's an earthquake?" Keko asked.

Do other parts
of the world have
earthquakes,
too?

Some earthquakes are strong enough to destroy large buildings.

Her dad sat down. "The earth has layers like an egg," he said. "The **core** of the earth is like the yolk. Around it, the **mantle** is melted rock. The shell of the earth is the **crust**. It is a thin outside layer of solid rock."

An earthquake is the sudden movement of part of the earth's crust. The epicenter is the area directly above the place where an earthquake starts.

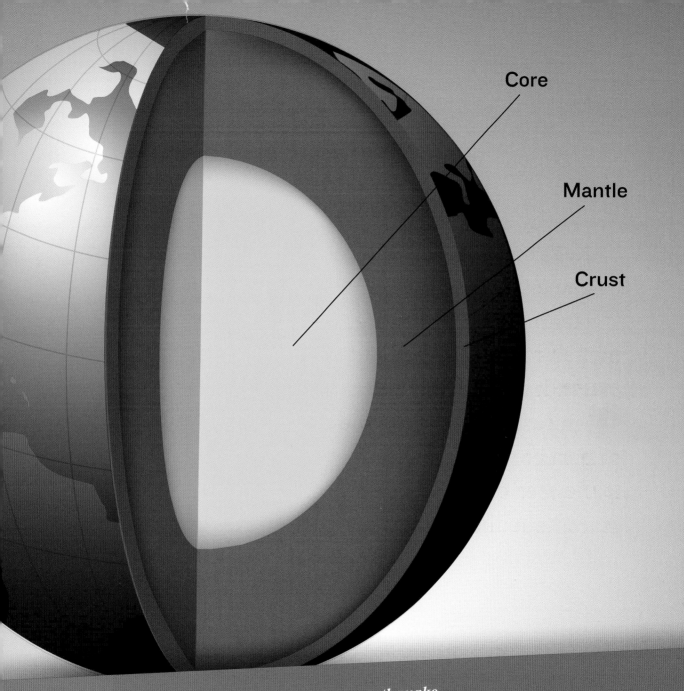

Core

Mantle

Crust

When the earth's crust moves, we call it an earthquake.

Plates and Faults

Keko was worried. "We never had an earthquake before."

Her dad gave her a hug. "Most earthquakes in our country happen on the West Coast."

"But we don't live on the West Coast," said Keko.

"Sometimes earthquakes happen in other places, too," he said. "Most earthquakes are mild. We don't even feel them."

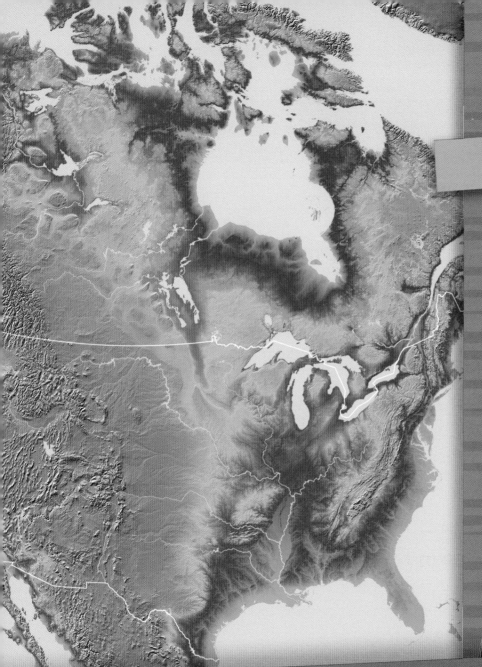

LOOK!

Can you find the West Coast on this map?

Do you live an area where earthquakes happen often?

The earth's crust is broken into pieces called **plates**. Most earthquakes happen along **fault lines**. These are places where two plates meet.

The San Andreas Fault runs along the West Coast. It's where the **North American Plate** and the **Pacific Plate** meet.

The San Andreas Fault is part of the Ring of Fire. This is a circle around the Pacific Plate. Almost all earthquakes happen in this ring.

When the earth's plates move they can lift large rocks.

Measuring Quakes

"But what makes an earthquake?" asked Keko.

"The plates of the earth's crust move around," said Dad. "But their edges are rough. They can get stuck while the rest of the plate keeps moving. When that happens, energy gets stored."

Her dad got a rubber band and stretched it. "When enough energy is stored, it does this." He let the rubber band snap. "With a fault, the edge

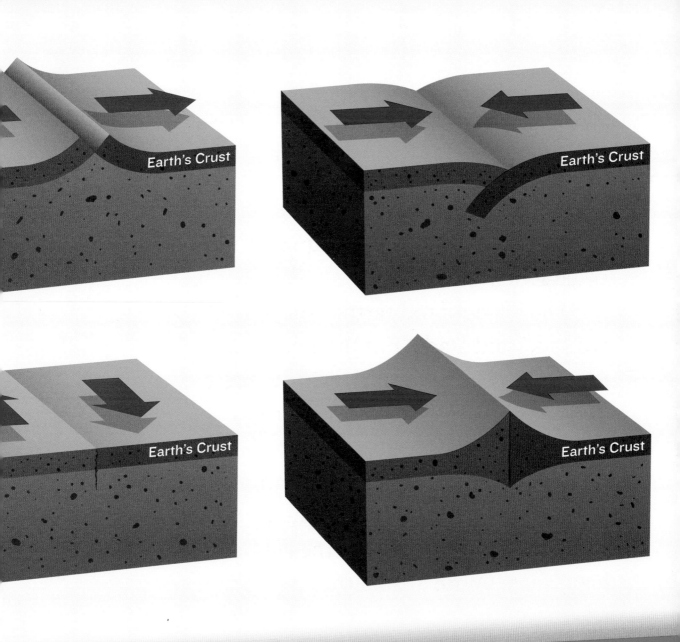

Earth's Crust

Earth's Crust

Earth's Crust

Earth's Crust

During an earthquake plates can be forced to move in different directions.

suddenly shifts," he said. "The energy ripples out in waves. The waves shake the ground. This is an earthquake."

Scientists measure earthquakes and **aftershocks** using the **Richter scale**. Most earthquakes are less than 3 on the Richter scale. We can hardly feel them. Earthquakes larger than 6 are strong. They can cause a lot of damage. Buildings can fall down. Roads can be damaged. People can be hurt or killed.

SEISMOGRAPH 23-4

SEISMOGRAPH 67RT23

SEISMOGRAPH 23-4

BLIP TRANCEIVER B67

SEISMOGRAPH 23-4

X432

ASK QUESTIONS

Ask a teacher or librarian to help you find out when the Richter scale was invented.

Scientists use this seismograph to measure earthquakes.

Being Prepared

"Can scientists tell when there will be an earthquake?" asked Keko.

"No," said Dad. "But they can tell where earthquakes are likely. That helps keep people safe. Builders can make buildings strong enough to stay up in an earthquake."

"What should we do if we have a powerful earthquake here?" asked Keko.

"Let's look online," said Dad.

Earthquakes can cause very large cracks in roads.

They found a Web site with safety tips. During an earthquake:

- Drop to the ground. Take cover under a sturdy table or desk. Hang on.

- Stay away from windows, outside walls, and anything that can fall on you.

- If you are in bed, stay there. Cover your head with your pillow.

- Do not go outside until the shaking stops.

- If you are outside, stay there. Get away from buildings, poles, and wires.

Specially trained dogs use their sense of smell to help rescuers find people after an earthquake.

Duffy was still hiding under the table. Keko petted him. "You knew just what to do during an earthquake!"

Keko picked up her glass. "Can earthquakes shake water, too?"

"**Tsunamis** are big waves caused by undersea earthquakes," said Dad. "Tsunamis can cause a lot of damage."

Keko wiped the table. "I'm glad our earthquake just spilled my milk. But now I know what to do if we have a big earthquake."

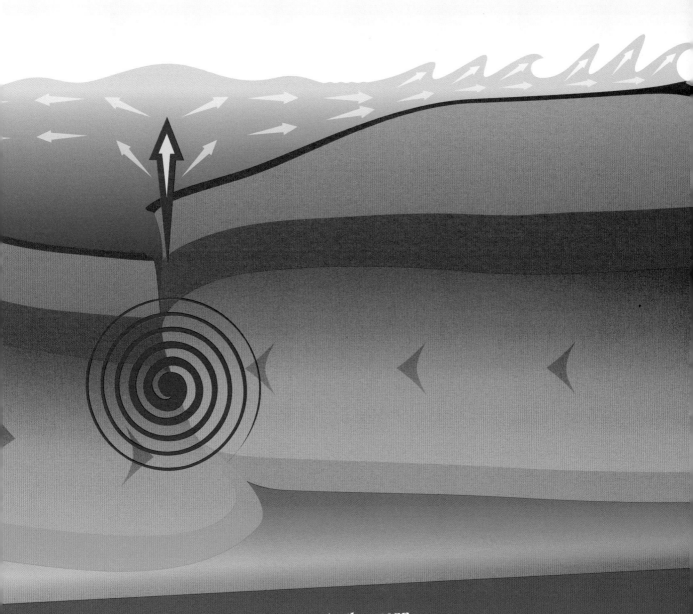

Earthquakes can happen on land and in the ocean.

Think About It

Do you know someone who has experienced an earthquake? Ask them how it felt. Compare his or her experience with the experience of Keko and her family.

Find another book or Web site with information about earthquakes. Is the information the same or different from the information in this book?

Talk with your parents or teachers about what to do if there is an earthquake near you. Make a list of what you can do to keep yourself safe.

Glossary

aftershocks (AF-tur-shokss) small earthquakes that come soon after a stronger earthquake in the same place

core (KOHR) the solid center of the earth

crust (KRUHST) the rocky outer shell of the earth

fault lines (FAWLT LINEZ) places where two of earth's plates meet

mantle (MAN-tuhl) the earth's middle layer of melted rock

North American Plate (NAWRTH uh-MER-i-kuhn PLEYT) the earth's plate under North America

Pacific Plate (puh-SIF-ik PLEYT) the earth's plate under the Pacific Ocean

plates (PLEYTS) pieces of the earth's crust

Richter scale (RIK-tur skeyl) the scale used to measure the strength of earthquakes

tsunamis (soo-NAH-meez) waves caused by an undersea earthquake

Find Out More

Books:

Anniss, Matt. *The Science of Earthquakes*. New York: Gareth Stevens, 2013.

McLeish, Ewan. *Earthquakes in Action*. New York: Rosen Publishing Group, 2009.

Park, Louise. *Earthquakes*. North Mankato, MN: Smart Apple Media, 2007.

Web Sites:

Earthquake and Hazards Program—Learn About Quakes and be Prepared
  http://quake.abag.ca.gov/students
  Learn even more about earthquakes, take a quiz, and complete a crossword puzzle.

FEMA—Ready: Be a Hero!
  www.ready.gov/kids
  This site helps kids and families prepare for a disaster.

Weather Wiz Kids—Earthquakes
  www.weatherwizkids.com/weather-earthquake.htm
  Find a link to science fair project ideas on this web site that relate to earthquakes.

Index

About the Author

Linda Crotta Brennan has a master's degree in education. She spent her life around books, teaching, and working at the library. Now she's a full time writer who loves learning new things. She lives with her husband and golden retriever. She has three grown daughters and a growing gaggle of grandchildren.